A LIFE
IN
EDUCATION

ANECDOTES

DEBORA RESNICK

AOS Publishing, 2024

Copyright © 2024

Debora Resnick

ISBN: 978-1-990496-93-6

Cover Design: Jessica James

Visit AOS Publishing's website:
www.aospublishing.com

CONTENTS

Introduction 1

Lightbulb Moment 2

If Only… 5

Thanks A Lot 6

No 8

College-Level 10

Uh-Oh 12

A Maieutic Moment 14

Turning Point 16

Let It Go 19

Words 21

Confidence 26

Wise Beyond Their Years 28

Oops 31

My Kind of Student 33

Parents 35

Confused 49

Conflicted 52

Except for Elizabeth 55

Stock-taking 57

Stock-taken 61

Anything But 65

Lost? 67

The Trades 72

History 78

I'm Not Motivated 81

Maturity 87

Posture 89

Different Folks 94

Perfectionist 108

Scarred 112

Time's Up 114

Oh, Dear 117

Haircut 119

Kindred Spirit 121

Thinking Ahead 123

Guardian Angels 125

Kudos 129

Epilogue 134

INTRODUCTION

Unlike universities, where faculty serve as advisors to students in matters academic, this task was assigned to a distinctive category of employees in the Quebec CEGEP (junior college) system: academic advisors.

The majority of exchanges that advisors have with students are mundane and repetitive. They entail explanations regarding the structure of their CEGEP program to students, how to plan their forthcoming semesters' courses, and if the student is interested in attending university, how to go about applying and what to expect.

Along the way, of course, the odd exchange with a student ends up having a special quality. The exchanges that follow had that quality and are the ones that stayed in the author's mind.

LIGHTBULB MOMENT

When Myra first started working as an academic advisor at Clarke College she worked in both the day division of the College and the evening division.

Eunice came to see Myra because she had previously been in the day division, where she had been in the nursing program, but had done poorly. She was attending evening classes to upgrade her academics in order to return to the nursing program in the day.

After discussing the number of courses Eunice had taken and whether the results she had obtained in them were sufficient, Myra asked what she thought was a perfectly innocent question: "Well, you've been out of nursing for two years now, what have you been doing?"

"Odd jobs here and there. I want to get back into school during the day."

"I can see that; you wouldn't be taking evening courses if you didn't. And you've done quite well."

"Thank you."

And because Myra knew that Eunice's readmission to the Nursing program was far from certain, she tried to keep the conversation going. "So, tell me, why do you want to be a nurse?"

Eunice looked at Myra but did not say anything.

Hmm, Myra thought, was her question more difficult than she had assumed?

Eunice continued to look at Myra in silence.

Myra waited.

And then Eunice's face took on a look of wonder. "You know what," she said, as she finally broke her silence. "I don't want to be a nurse." And now her words came rushing out: "In fact, I never wanted to be a nurse, my mother is the one who wanted me to be a nurse.

"And you know what else, I never even asked myself the question, I just went into nursing unthinkingly.

"But I don't want to be a nurse," Eunice stated again with the utmost firmness.

"And I'm not going back into Nursing," Eunice continued. "I even know what I want to do; I love languages, I'm going to go back to day school to study languages—

"Oh, my goodness," Eunice caught her breath and smiled broadly.

"In that case." Myra smiled right back. "Let's make a new plan." She flipped to the languages program grid in her program binder and began to explain the ins and outs of the program to Eunice.

IF ONLY...

One evening, a young man came to see Myra. He was working in construction and wanted to know how to become a chef. He hated what he was doing, he had always loved cooking and had recently decided it was time to make a change.

Nothing remotely connected to the restaurant or hospitality industry was taught at Clarke College, and Myra gave the young man the names of schools where he could get the training he was looking for.

A week later, another young man came to see Myra. He worked as a short-order cook and was totally fed up with the hours, with the pressure, with the smells. He hated what he was doing and was looking for something totally different, preferably physical work, outdoor work, maybe even something in construction…

THANKS A LOT

There was a difference between Clarke's daytime and evening student body. The former was more homogeneous, since the pre-university programs, which constituted about three quarters of the daytime student body, was made up almost exclusively of students coming to college straight from high school, while the evening division was more heterogeneous and attracted a greater percentage of older students.

It was not unusual for Myra to encounter women in their late thirties and early forties who, having stayed home to raise their children, wanted to go back to school and train for a career.

Social Work was one of those careers, and these students came to Myra after having called McGill and having been told that to be eligible as a mature student they needed some exposure to the field and needed to have passed a few courses at Clarke—English, of course, and any two or three other social science courses.

Nothing was said about the extent or type of exposure they were expected to have had to the field, nor the level at which they were expected to perform in the few courses they were being asked to take.

Myra felt that it would be remiss on her part not to provide such students with a little more information, especially if they happened to have brought their high school record and she saw especially poor grades in a curriculum composed of a minimum number of easy credits.

Wanting to better oneself was laudable; being led to believe that it was going to be easy was not.

It was even worse for those students who, in their thirties or forties, wanted to go into a career in science.

Oh, they were missing one calculus course and two college-level science courses, they were told by whomever they happened to speak to at McGill.

Thank you, again, Myra thought as she began to explain to the student in her office that science was like a language, that you couldn't take advanced Spanish without having first passed the beginner's and intermediate levels. The course of action was similar with math and science. First the high school levels in these disciplines had to be passed before one could undertake calculus and science at the college-level…

NO

Late one afternoon, Myra received a call from an evening female student—the voice was unusually flat and expressionless—asking whether Clarke offered a law program.

"No, we don't offer law as such, but we have a course called Business Law, and in the day division we have a three-year program that can train you to be a legal secretary."

"You don't have a law program?"

"No, we do not."

Six months later, Myra received a call from the same student— she recognized the voice, the same flatness, the same expressionlessness—asking whether Clarke had a law program.

This time Myra decided she had best explain the whole procedure. "If you mean a program to become a lawyer, no, we don't. You can only train to become a lawyer at the university level. If that's what you want to do you have to get a university degree first and then apply to law school.

"We have programs at Clarke that can help you get to university, but mature students—students over a certain age—are eligible to attend university without having to complete college. For example, Concordia University has a special program for mature students. Even McGill accepts mature students, but they want to see a few college courses passed first, for example English, Humanities, the odd social science course. We have these courses here in the evening. You can even take a Business Law course here.

"But law, the program to become a lawyer, is offered only at university, at McGill in English, and at both the University of Montreal and at the University of Quebec at Montreal in French.

"We have a few French courses in the evening, so we can help a little if your French is weak, otherwise you might check out second-language   French courses offered at the University of Montreal. They have every level of both oral and written French.

"I hope all this helps."

Six months later, Myra received a call from the same student—oh, that voice—asking whether Clarke had a law program. By now Myra had learned exactly how to handle her caller. "No, we do not," she replied, and replaced the receiver.

COLLEGE-LEVEL

~~~

Myra had never given it much thought while she had worked in the admissions department. The requirement to get into CEGEP was a high school diploma. But this requirement suddenly made more sense after Myra met with Eileen Carter.

Eileen was enrolled in one of Clarke's abbreviated evening programs, the Attestation in Early Childhood Education.

Eileen came to see Myra after she passed the first three courses of the Attestation, two practical, hands-on courses dealing with health and safety in a daycare, and a third, very basic psychology course. It was the fourth course, Observing and Reporting, that Eileen was having difficulty with. She had failed it twice.

When Myra looked up Eileen's academic record, she found that Eileen had never finished high school; that in fact, she had left school in the middle of grade nine.
~~~

Observing and Reporting, as the title conveyed, was a course in which the student learned to observe what was going on in a daycare and describe what they saw to others.

Of course, in order to accurately describe what one saw, one had to know how to distinguish between accident and aggression, between annoyance and anger, between shyness and fear, between tears of frustration and tears of pain—but what if one did not possess the vocabulary with which to do this?

There was an insurmountable gulf between Eileen's ambition and her lack of schooling, Myra realized. Maybe finishing high school would never have made Eileen the sharpest of observers, but surely it would have given her more of the vocabulary she needed with which to think. She may have gained the skills to put into words what she had observed and communicate this to others so as to get feedback and constructive criticism, in order to ultimately learn to practice the profession effectively.

Myra recommended that Eileen go back to finish high school.

And, of course, she also saw to it that the requirement for admission to the Attestation was changed so that henceforth all entrants to the program possessed a high school diploma.

UH-OH

Uh-oh, Myra thought after Giles Cochrane left her office; she was not prepared to give up flying, but what he had said was pretty scary.

Tall, well-dressed, and well-spoken, Giles was a former air traffic controller who had quit and was looking for something else to do.

"I thought this was a dream job," Myra said. "It's well-paying, secure. The training is demanding, from what I heard, but otherwise—"

"It's a gruelling job," Giles said. "First of all, it's shift work, so it takes a toll on you and your family. But that's not why I quit. I quit because of the cowboys out there."

"The cowboys?" Myra asked.

"Yes, the cowboys, the pilots—not all, of course, but the few out there—who think we're namby-pambies because we insist they follow our instructions, who think flying is a game, even though they're flying airplanes full of people…"

A MAIEUTIC MOMENT

The student was very upset. She had received a grade of eighty-seven on her exam but felt she should have received a ninety-two. "I want to register a complaint against Mrs. Boyer. I did not get credit for one of my homework assignments. She asks us to bring them up to her desk and show them to her. She glances at them and records the five marks in her register. I know she missed mine because I always do my homework, and the way I calculate it, that's where I'm missing five marks."

"Did you discuss this with her?" Myra asked.

"Yes," the student replied. "But she brushed me off. I want to register a complaint. How do I go about doing it?"

"Let me speak to her. I'll see what I can do."

Mrs. Boyer had a good reputation; she was a little hasty in her judgements, but she was a conscientious, dedicated teacher. Myra was sure a formal complaint would not be necessary.

And, sure enough, when she told Mrs. Boyer why she was calling, Mrs. Boyer was a little put out. "No student has ever complained about me," she said.

"I think the matter can easily be cleared up," Myra said. She proceeded to describe what the student thought had happened. "It seems you ask the students to show you their homework assignments."

"Yes."

"How do they do this?"

"By coming up to my desk and showing them to me."

"One at a time or in a group?"

"In a…" And Mrs. Boyer hesitated. "It could be that I missed hers…"

"Yes, that's most probably what happened."

TURNING POINT

Even though Myra had had lots of experience in education before becoming an academic advisor, for the first five years on the job, Myra did not feel she was on solid ground.

Of course, if she was not sure of something, she checked with her more experienced colleagues, but, as she explained to one of her colleagues, admissions were circumscribed. Most Clarke students came from Quebec, and for those who didn't, there were reference books one could use, government resources one could consult to figure out the educational system from which a student came and extrapolate to CEGEP.

But in advising, while most questions had to do with the requirements of the various programs Clarke offered, she never knew when a student might ask a question to which she did not know the answer, or, worse, when she might give the wrong answer to a question, advising being so open-ended, the needs of students being so fluid, the whole process being, essentially, a work in progress.

And so it was that, after about five years into the job, Myra was working with a student who had set her mind on going into business but whose grades overall and mathematics grades in particular were not sufficient to be admitted to a business program at university.

Round and round they had gone, about how to upgrade overall, about how to upgrade in mathematics—an absolute prerequisite to the program—about how, whichever way they looked at it, the student's lack of ability in math was going to impede her.

About five minutes before their time was up and for the first time since she had become an advisor, Myra stopped following an imagined script, stepped out of what she thought was her role, and asked a seemingly non-academic question, the question of an interested, curious, fellow human being. "Tell me, something, Christina, if you were totally free, if you were to close your eyes and dream about your ideal job, about what you would really like to do, what would that be?"

Christina did not have to close her eyes, as she knew the answer to that question right away, and her face, which throughout her appointment had been closed and tight, broke into the broadest of smiles.

Myra was completely taken aback. The contrast between their difficult, uphill conversation—it had seemed as if they had been climbing an insurmountable mountain for twenty-five minutes—and the transformation in Christina that had just taken place before her eyes meant that there was only one thing to do: tell the student what she had just seen. "Christina, I wish you could see your face, I wish you could see your smile. I am not telling you what to do, I am just telling you what I just saw: a smile that changed you, that relaxed you, that freed you. Now it's for you to decide what you want to do with that smile."

That smile freed Myra as well. It was the first time she had allowed herself a personal comment, and the result had been transformative for her, too, because suddenly, she felt on more solid ground. She had not really been sure of her role before and had held herself back because of it. Now she knew what she had to do: she had to be fully there for the students, and that included being fully herself, with her judgement, with her experience and insight. She had to be more spontaneous with them, allow herself the odd personal comment. If the idea was to help them, that, too, would help them, give them something meaningful to hold onto, something that might make a difference in their lives.

LET IT GO

Had Myra not had that experience with Christina, she would never have allowed herself this gesture with Domenica.

Domenica came to see Myra because she had a dilemma. Domenica had completed two years of a three-year program and had come to realize that the program was not for her. Friends were telling her she was crazy, she had one year left to do, that she should finish the program. Her husband was telling her the same thing. Her mother was telling her the same thing.

"Do you want me to tell you the same thing?" Myra asked.

"No, I want you to tell me what you think," Domenica said.

"I think you are a mature adult, that you have been doing well in the program, and that if you realize now that the program is not for you and that you have no intention of working in the field—

"Am I right in that?" Myra interrupted herself. "Am I correct in saying that you have no intention of working in the field?"

"Yes, that's right," Domenica replied.

"Then, I agree with you, let it go."

Domenica's face relaxed into a smile. "Thank you. At last someone who heard what I said."

Then Myra thought of something. She reached for a piece of paper and wrote out a sentence. "Here, Domenica, here's a little present for you."

On the paper Myra wrote out a sentence by George Eliot that she had read years ago and that had been pivotal in her life at the time: "constancy in error is constancy in folly".

It took Dominica a minute to grasp what Myra had written, then she smiled broadly. "I love it," she said, and she folded the paper and put it in her purse. "Thank you. Thank you very much."

WORDS

English used to be but no longer was the mother tongue of the majority of Clarke's student body. But Clarke was an English college, so all the students who frequented the place spoke English, although the grammar of many students was faulty and the vocabulary of the vast majority limited.

When Myra moved to advising, she knew enough to adapt what she had to say to whomever she was speaking. To the mature Chinese student whose English was at the minimum level for admission but who got hundreds in his accounting courses, and to the newly-arrived Russian student hoping to get into Clarke's Nursing program, Myra slowed down and spoke in monosyllables to ensure that the information and instructions she was conveying were fully understood.

► Whimsical

Thus it was with joy that Myra heard an excellent student with grades good enough to be admitted to pre-medicine at McGill ask whether it was whimsical of him to want to take the year off before commencing his medical studies. He wanted to do some travelling before settling down to the grind he knew awaited him and wondered what she thought.

Go for it, Myra thought, based on that word alone—go for it!

► Epiphany

A few months later, a student in Clarke's language program came to Myra to announce that she had had an epiphany and realized she wanted to go into linguistics. The question was, how was she to go about it?

Two days later, another student from the same program also reported having had an epiphany. She, too, wanted to go into linguistics.

Two students in the same week, both using the word epiphany, both wanting to study linguistics, what was going on? Myra pulled out her program binder and flipped to the languages grid, and there was her answer. This was the semester in which students took The Story of Language, a course taught by Jean-François Roussel, the program coordinator. Was it also a coincidence that Jean-François had recently won Clarke's Excellence in Teaching award? And that, while accepting the award, Jean-François recounted that he had once had a nightmare in which he had been on his way to Clarke and had dreamt that he had to get a real job?

▶ Intercourse

Of course, sometimes students slipped, as when they referred to an intersession course—Myra had heard this on at least five different occasions—as an inter-course.

▶ Affection

One of the more amusing exchanges, in Myra's judgement, was when a student sat down opposite her and announced that he needed affection—

Affection? Whatever did the student mean?

But the student was holding a transcript from an American college and pointing to the economics course he had passed there—

Ah, the student was inquiring about getting an equivalence—

Myra had not been able to resist saying, "We all do" before proceeding to deal with the student's request.

▶Awesome

And then there was the best definition of 'awesome' Myra would ever hear.

Early in the 1990s, a group of bridging courses in mathematics and science courses was created to help students transition between studying science in high school and studying science in CEGEP.

Then, for a two-year period in the mid-nineties, these bridging courses were retired. Clarke continued to offer these courses, but they no longer counted for credit. They were imposed on students for the same reason they had originally been created, to help students with weaknesses in their math/science background succeed at college.

Two years later, however, these courses were resuscitated under a new guise and were again deemed credit-worthy.

Daniel had been admitted to Clarke College during the two-year period when the courses did not count. He had not graduated by the time these courses had begun to count again, so when he sat down in front of Myra to register for summer school, he fully expected to register for two advanced science courses during the shortened summer semester ahead of him. With two such science courses to take, Daniel was going to have six hours of very tough science classes per day, four days a week for the next six and a half weeks.

Unknown to Daniel, the advising staff at Clarke had decided to disregard the two-year hiatus imposed on the credit-worthiness of those bridging courses, judging that if they had once carried credit and did so again, they should never have stopped carrying credit.

Myra took one look at Daniel's transcript and said as much to him.

"You're kidding me," Daniel said, leaning forward in his chair.

"No, I'm serious," Myra replied.

"You're kidding me," Daniel said again, leaning further forward in his chair.

"No, I'm serious."

"You're kidding me," Daniel said a third time, still unable to believe what he was hearing.

"It didn't make sense," Myra explained. "The same courses counted once upon a time, then they stopped counting, and then they started counting again. So we decided—"

At which point Daniel leaned back in his chair, threw back his head and cried, "Awesome."

"Awesome," Daniel cried again, as he raised his hands and pumped his fists in the air.

"Awesome," Daniel cried yet again. Then he jumped up from his chair. "I don't know how to thank you," he said. "Oh, my god, oh, my god," he mumbled as he picked up his transcript, grabbed his backpack, and raced out of the room.

CONFIDENCE

A majority of students worried about their future.

Myra had worked at Clarke long enough to have lived through many economic cycles. When the economy was booming, there were jobs. When there was a downturn, jobs dried up. When there was an extended downturn, Clarke's enrolment went up as people returned to school in the hope of improving their employment chances.

But the odd student did not doubt him or herself.

▶ Kyle

Kyle came to see Myra in the middle of a severe recession. It was the early nineties; the economy was in the doldrums and had been for months. Kyle had come to get information about how to become a high school teacher.

After Myra gave Kyle the information, she couldn't help commenting, "I've met quite a few students who were interested in teaching, but most of them wouldn't commit to a four-year university program because they were afraid they wouldn't find a position when they graduated."

Kyle locked eyes with Myra. "I'll find a job," he said quietly.

▶ Sylvia

Sylvia came to see Myra during that same recession. She wanted to know what to study at university in order to become an art curator.

Myra gave Sylvia the information she was looking for. "It will take a master's degree, not just a bachelor's degree to get there," Myra said. "So you're looking at quite a bit of schooling. Are you ready for that?"

"Yes, I am."

"Of course, along the way, you should try to pick up some experience as a volunteer, and then as you progress in your studies and if you're lucky—because times are tough—you'll even be able to pick up some part-time work. But, I have to emphasize, times are tough and the art business is a very tough field to break into—"

"I know," Sylvia said firmly. "But this is what I want to do and I will do it."

WISE BEYOND
THEIR YEARS

$\sim\!\sim$

▶ Vicky

One of the stories Myra liked to tell students with whom she discussed careers was a story she brought with her from her experience as admissions coordinator.

Times were tough, extremely so—it was the early eighties—and in addition to her duties dealing with admissions requests, Myra also handled all program transfer requests. The request form was straightforward but happened to include a space in which students could make comments and explain why they wanted the change they were asking for.

Most students left the space blank. If they had started in science and were asking to change to business, it was clear that they had realized science was not for them. Or if they had started in one of

Clarke's three-year programs and were asking to change to a two-year program, they had realized that their three-year program was not for them.

Myra did not remember whether, when Vicky asked to change from her two-year communications program to Clarke's three-year animal health program, she had written anything in that space. Given the times, a three-year program that would train her to work as a veterinary assistant made a heck of a lot more sense than a communications program that lead to further study in areas fraught with dire job opportunities.

But a year later Vicky was back. This time when she filed her transfer request, she did write something in the space provided for comments: "If I'm going to be unemployed, I might as well be unemployed in the field that I love."

▶ Kristen

Kristen said something that it had taken Myra years to figure out—that if you can't imagine doing something, you don't really want to do it.

When discussing various career choices, those were the very words Kristen used: "I can't imagine doing that for the rest of my life."

At which point Myra asked Kristen whether she would like to hear a story illuminating that very point. "Of course" was the answer, and so Myra proceeded to tell it.

Years earlier, she had asked a Clarke faculty member who taught physics how he had come to develop a special course for music students called The Physics of Music.

Ah, the teacher had replied, that was easy, he had been playing the oboe since his youth and got together regularly with other amateur musicians to play chamber music.

The interesting thing, the teacher had gone on to say, was that when he was in high school, he could not make up his mind between a career in physics or music, but he had chosen physics because he could not imagine making a living in music. So there he was, teaching physics at Clarke.

The really amusing thing, the teacher had then concluded his story, was that he had a friend who had had the same dilemma, but he had not been able to imagine making a living in physics, so he had chosen music and had ended up becoming a music professor.

OOPS

Advising appointments are scheduled by the half-hour. Jonathan was about ten minutes late for his appointment, and being a polite young man, apologized as soon as he arrived. "Sorry, Miss, I had to take my mother to the hospital. She wasn't feeling well, she's fifty-six, she's old, you know."

Myra ushered Jonathan into her office where she proceeded to answer his questions and explain whatever needed explaining. "Is there anything else I can help you with?" Myra asked when they were done.

"Thanks, Miss, no, that was very helpful."

"Glad to help, Jonathan."

Jonathan got up to leave.

"By the way, Jonathan, this is neither here nor there, but I just thought I'd mention, I'm sixty-two."

Jonathan's face fell. "Oh, my god, Miss, I'm so sorry. I didn't mean…"

MY KIND OF STUDENT

Anthony called with a question during registration.

While checking his file, Myra saw that Anthony's English placement test results had not been entered in his file. This meant that Anthony could not register for his first required English course.

"I'll call you right back, Anthony," Myra said. She called the person in charge and got the information she was looking for.

Myra called Anthony back with the results. But then she noticed that his French placement results had not been entered either. "I'll call you right back, Anthony."

Myra called the person in charge and called Anthony back.

Anthony now had another question. Myra was not sure of the response. "Sorry, I have to check with your coordinator. I'm not sure whether I can do that."

The coordinator was in her office, and again, Myra was able to call Anthony back right away. "Hi, Anthony, it's me, Myra."

"Are we dating?" Anthony asked without a moment's hesitation.

Myra burst out laughing. "It sure does sound like it, doesn't it?"

Myra told the story to Jean-Francois Roussel when she next saw him. Jean Francois let out a loud guffaw. "Now that's the kind of student I love to have in my class," he said.

PARENTS

Once, while Myra had been admissions coordinator, she had met the parents of a refused applicant and their son. At one point during the meeting, the father switched to Yiddish to say something to the applicant's mother. For a second Myra had been tempted to join in the conversation, but decided there was no point and continued to listen to their conversation without letting on that she understood every word they were saying.

As an advisor, Myra also met with parents and offspring occasionally, and although she never heard Yiddish spoken again, the dynamics between parent and child or parents and child always became clear almost as soon as they entered Myra's office, as clear as if they were speaking a secret language between them they thought she did not understand.

▶ Mrs. Chen

Mrs. Chen was a striking woman. She was beautifully coiffed and expensively dressed, and had come to see Myra about her son, James. She was accompanied by a man who was also well-groomed and expensively dressed, but who was clearly not James' father.

James was not doing well at Clarke. He had attended a private high school and had done reasonably well there, but he was barely passing his courses at Clarke.

Mrs. Chen began by telling Myra how she had founded her own business and was running it very successfully, that there was a place for her son in the business and that all she wanted was for him to get some business training and he would have it made, but she just couldn't get through to him.

James listened impassively to everything his mother said and did not utter a word.

At one point, Myra turned to James and asked him whether he had used the various resources Clarke had to help students who needed a little extra help—for example, the Math resource centre and the English resource centre. "Perhaps you can book an appointment with me in a day or two and you and I could make a plan," she suggested.

"I'll book it on my way out," James said. "I have to go now, I have a class." And James left the room.

The man also got up and excused himself. What had been the point of his being there, Myra wondered, was he Mrs. Chen's current husband, or, more likely, current boyfriend?

But now Mrs. Chen turned to Myra and said, "So, what do you think of my son, the loser? I don't know what I'm going to do with him."

▶ Mrs. Vellupillai

It happened that Myra's very next appointment that morning was with another mother and son. Fabien had also run into problems and Mrs. Vellupillai had come to try to get a better understanding of what this meant for his future. "Fabien does not keep things from me, he tells me everything," the mother said, and she turned to her son and smiled. "But we are not from here." She turned back to Myra. "And I just want to understand the system better. We don't have CEGEPs back home..."

▶ The Palermos

Mr. and Mrs. Palermo came to see Myra with their son Carlo. Carlo had not done particularly well in high school and was not doing particularly well at Clarke, either.

Myra explained that if Carlo did not pass the minimum number of courses in his current semester, he would be obliged to leave the day division and be forced to upgrade in the evening division if he ever wanted to be readmitted to day studies.

"What do you mean?" Mr. Palermo asked.

"What's the matter with you?" Mrs. Palermo turned on her husband. "Can't you understand plain English? Carlo will be kicked out of day school and have to take courses at night.

"Can he take the same courses at night?" Mrs. Palermo turned to Myra. "Can he continue his program at night?"

"No," Myra replied. "We have general courses at night, we don't have his program courses at night."

"So why are you—?"

"Oh, shut up, Paulo." Mrs. Palermo turned to her husband. "They don't have the same courses at night, okay?"

This went on for about twenty minutes.

▶ Mr. Winston

Mr. Winston had come to see Myra about his son, Brian.

"Hi," Myra said as she ushered Brian and his dad into her small office. She pointed to the two chairs in front of her desk.

Mr. Winston closed the door to her office, firmly took hold of one of the visitors' chairs, and moved it over as close as he could to the wall on his left and sat down.

Brian took hold of his chair, and just as firmly, moved it over as close to the wall on his right and sat down.

Myra barely had time to digest this when Mr. Winston launched into his tirade.

"I don't know what I am going to do. Brian is lost, he has no idea what to do with himself, he is not studying, I can tell, he can't possibly be keeping up in his courses, he lies to me, he told me he would be taking math here and he isn't—"

"Excuse me for a minute, Mr. Winston." Myra looked at Brian. "Did you try to take Math here? Were you told by your high school counsellor that you would be able to take math here?"

"Yes," Brian replied.

"So what happened?"

"There was no room in the course."

Myra turned to Mr. Winston. "This happens all the time," she said. "The high schools restrict access to math and science courses in order to improve their success rates and tell students that they will be able to get those courses at CEGEP—this has been going on for years. Well, we're not a high school and cannot accommodate all the students who come here looking for these courses. Brian, like many other students, was misinformed by his high school."

"Okay, fine, but did he come and talk to you or one of your colleagues when he didn't get the course, did he take the trouble to inform himself how to do that? No, I had to insist that he make an appointment to come and see one of you, that's why I'm here, to inform myself, because I can't trust Brian to do that, let alone figure out what he wants to do. He's lost, and I would be sympathetic if he cared, but he doesn't seem to care. I'm here because I don't know what to do. I know how important it is to get a good education. It's not like I have a business which Brian can go into; I'm an accountant, and I can see how tough things are out there."

"I can help a little with that," Myra said, and turned to Brian. She looked away immediately, as the boy seemed near tears and any sympathy on her part would be fatal to him. She addressed herself to Mr. Winston. "We have counsellors here who do career workshops, who administer interest tests that can help students find a direction—"

"Excuse me." Brian stood up. "I…I need to go to the bathroom," he said, and Brian left the room.

"What am I going to do?" Mr. Winston looked at Myra beseechingly. "I am beside myself with worry, and he just doesn't get it."

"I can see that you're concerned, and I can see why, but may I make a suggestion?"

"Sure, anything."

"I think it would be a good idea if I spoke to Brian alone. I'll explain the interest test, I'll discuss the math with him, but—"

"Great idea. Yes. He's not a bad kid, but I'm so frustrated." Mr. Winston stood up and put on his coat. "Yes, please, talk to him. Here's my phone number, in case you want to talk to me—"

"And here's my card." Myra handed Mr. Winston her card.

"Yes, thanks," he said, and Mr. Winston rushed out.

Brian returned about a minute later. "Where's my father?" he asked in a panic as he came in and saw that his father was gone.

"I suggested he leave, that it would be best—"

"I have to say goodbye—" he said, and Brian ran out to look for him, and returned a minute later.

"He did not leave because he was angry, Brian, I can assure you. Now, let's get down to business. How are you doing in your courses?"

"I'm not doing well. I'm failing two, I'mm borderline in two, and I'm passing English and Physical Education."

"But you have to pass four to stay out of trouble. Have you told your father?"

"Are you kidding me? He would kill me."

"If I were you, Brian, I would tell him now. First of all, I would want to get it out of my system. But I also think it would show your father that you're taking responsibility—"

"There's no way I'm telling him now. I'll tell him just before the letter comes—"

"And you'll be able to sleep, you'll be able to go about your business—"

"Trust me, I will. It's better than having him at me for the next three weeks."

Myra was not convinced and showed by her expression that she wasn't.

"Trust me, Miss," Brian said. "I've learned my lesson. I realized three weeks ago I was in trouble and I didn't like it one bit."

"Meaning?"

"I won't let it happen again."

Myra studied the boy for a minute. "Okay, I believe you. But if what you're saying is true, then telling your father now would be a good thing to do. Tell him what you just told me—"

"No way, Miss, no way. I know you're trying to help, but I know my dad."

▶ Mr. Persaud

Mohan's father came to see Myra with his son because Mohan wanted to change programs—Mohan was in the second year of a three-year business program—and Mr. Persaud did not understand why his son did not want to finish what he had started.

"He doesn't talk," Mr. Persaud said. "He doesn't tell us what's going on, and now, all of sudden, he wants to change programs. I don't understand such a thing." Mr. Persaud looked at Myra pleadingly. "He's the one who chose it, no one forced him into it, I don't understand."

"These things do happen, Mr. Persaud," she said, and Myra turned to Mohan. "Do you have any idea what you want to do?"

Mohan looked at Myra, looked at his father, looked back at Myra; he seemed to be struggling to say something, but he remained silent.

"Do you see what I mean?" Mr. Persaud said. "He doesn't talk. My wife says the same thing, he doesn't talk."

"Mr. Persaud, Mohan is not the first person to wake up and realize that the program he chose is not for him. Especially one of our three-year programs, as they do have a pretty narrow focus. It happens all the time. But—" She turned to Mohan again. "You must have an idea of what you like, of what you would like to study. Can you tell us what you have been thinking?"

This time the struggle to say something was etched even more deeply on Mohan's face, but still he remained silent.

"The lady can't help you if you don't speak, Mohan," Mr. Persaud addressed his son.

And, finally, Mohan let it out, but even then, only in a whisper: "History."

"I still think Mohan should finish what he started," Mr. Persaud said.

"Did I hear you say you liked history?" Myra asked.

"Yes," Mohan replied in the same whisper.

"Okay, then, Mohan," Myra summed things up. "Here's your choice. You can change into a two-year program in which you can take history courses—" Myra stopped to do the calculations on the notepaper in front of her—"Which will take you two semesters to complete, or you finish the program you're in, which, because it's a longer program, will take three semesters.

"One more thing, though—if you decide to go to university to study history, you are eligible whether you graduate in a two-year or three-year program. There are no specific courses you have to take at CEGEP to be eligible to study history at university. If you are a reader—" Myra looked Mohan in the eye— "Do you read the newspaper, for example, do you keep up with current events?"

"Yes," Mohan replied, and a faint smile appeared on his face.

"Good. So what do you think, do you want to finish your program or—"

"I think Mohan should finish what he started," Mr. Persaud interjected. "He's the one who chose it, you finish what you start—"

"I'll stay in my program and finish it," Mohan said.

"Okay, then," Myra said. "Follow the grid for your program." Myra reached for a file folder nearby, found a copy of the grid, and handed it to Mohan. "And come back and see me when you're about to finish. We can discuss university then."

"Thank you, Miss, thank you," Mr. Persaud reached out to shake Myra's hand. "I don't know how to thank you."

▶ Mrs. Huang

Annie came to see Myra before the semester was over, afraid she was failing her first-year Nursing course. Clarke's policy was clear: if you failed Nursing in your first semester, you could not continue in the program.

And what was worse, it was unlikely another college would accept a failing student into their Nursing program.

When Annie made a second appointment three weeks later and Myra checked her grades before ushering her into her office, she saw that Annie had, indeed, failed. When Myra went out to get her, Annie was there with her mother.

Myra ushered the two women into her office and turned to Annie. "I saw the results; what you were afraid would happen happened, I'm sorry."

"Thank you," Annie said evenly. "Is there anything I can do about it?"

"I'm afraid not, our policy is clear. And in case you think we are being hard-hearted, the policy is based on experience." Myra addressed both mother and daughter. "The number of students who fail their first Nursing course and then go on to graduate from the program is infinitesimal, and our policy is based on that fact."

"What about other colleges? If I go into another program and do well in it?" Annie asked.

"I can't answer for other colleges. But I know we don't accept students into our Nursing program who have failed elsewhere," Myra replied.

"Well, I was thinking, how do you become a consultant?"

"A consultant in what field?"

"In the medical field, between patient and the medical staff, for example."

"Well, hospitals, most large public institutions, have ombudspeople or public advocates."

"Do you have to be a lawyer?"

"Not necessarily. Clarke has a human rights officer, and she has a degree in Human Relations. We also have a student advocate; her background is in Social Work but she took training in conflict resolution."

"But as far as Nursing is concerned, you're saying it's over for me, is that right?"

"I'm afraid so, I'm sorry, but yes. Can you tell me what happened, Annie? Based on your high school grades, I would have expected you to succeed."

"I didn't work hard enough. I thought I could put in the same amount of work as I did in high school, which I found pretty easy—"

"I told her," Mrs. Huang, Annie's mother, interjected. "I could tell that she wasn't putting in enough effort. I graduated from Nursing here ten years ago, and I remember how hard I had to work. I even remember you, I came to see you once or twice."

"Really? I'm sorry, Mrs. Huang, I'm not that good with faces. So are you working as a nurse now?"

"Yes, in oncology at the new Glen hospital."

"Gosh, that must be tough?"

"Yes, but you can do so much good."

"I'm sure."

"And you learn a lot. I've learned not to get upset, not to get angry—"Mrs. Huang looked at Annie. "Years ago I would have been much less accepting, much more critical of Annie; I would have yelled, we would have fought, but I've learned you can't live like that, and it doesn't help anyway."

"You have a wise mom, Annie." Myra turned to the girl. "Okay, so let's look at what you can do next semester. Based on what you said, I would recommend you transfer into Social Science...."

CONFUSED

Poor Berenice had applied to four different universities, had been accepted by all four of them, and now she didn't know what to do.

"Which four, and which programs at the four?" Myra asked.

"I've been accepted to law at Université de Montréal and in business at McGill, Concordia, and HEC."

"Congratulations! And what seems to be the problem?"

"I don't know what to do, which university to go to, which program to go into."

"Well, I think you should scratch out law. Had you really wanted to become a lawyer you wouldn't have applied to law just at UdeM, you would also have applied to law at McGill and the other French universities. I'm guessing you wanted to know whether you would get accepted, and now you know."

The frown on Berenice's brow eased a little. "Yes, that's true. Okay, but that still leaves me with a dilemma."

"And what dilemma is that?"

"I don't know which to choose between McGill, Concordia, and HEC."

"Well, HEC is in French and the other two are in English," Myra said. "You could choose on that basis. Or you can choose based on which one is easier for you to get to, or to which one some of your friends are going—"

"To tell you the truth, I'm tempted by McGill but I'm afraid I'll find it too hard; after all, it's McGill…" Berenice's voice trailed off.

"And some of my friends are going to Concordia," Berenice continued. "I know their business school is good but McGill is still McGill, and they're a top university…

"I can get a scholarship at Concordia, so that's something, too…

"My mother went to McGill…

"But I'm worried that I'll find it too hard at McGill—"

"I think we can scratch HEC," Myra said.

Berenice looked at Myra in astonishment.

"Well," Myra explained. "You haven't mentioned HEC once in all of this debating back and forth. I think it's fair to say that HEC is not in the running."

"You're right," Berenice agreed readily. "Thanks."

"So now, about McGill and Concordia—I don't know why you're so worried about McGill. You're one of the stronger students they accepted—"

"You think so?"

"I know so. Their cut-off is approximately eighty percent, your average is over ninety—"

"But it's McGill; I don't know, I'm really afraid…"

"Okay, Berenice. Now it's time for me to call your attention to this little sign on my bulletin board." Myra pointed to the bottom right corner of the board. Berenice seemed to have trouble finding it so Myra read the text out loud: "I advise, you decide."

It took a moment for Berenice to get the point. And then she smiled. "I get it, you're not going to tell me which university to choose."

"That's right, I'm not. But I will say this one more time, don't let fear stop you from going to McGill. Now off you go. I'm confident you will succeed wherever you choose to go."

And Berenice left Myra's office with all traces of a frown gone from her face.

CONFLICTED

Sarah was not so much confused as conflicted. She could not make up her mind between going to university to study sociology, with which she had fallen in love at Clarke, or to study fashion at a local private college.

On the one hand, she wanted to go to university.

On the other hand, she wanted to study fashion. Her mother had been in the industry and it definitely attracted her.

But she really wanted to go to university. And she really loved sociology. She could always do fashion afterwards, right?

But fashion was practical, and much as she loved sociology, she was not going to become an academic, because what could she do with sociology other than teach it?

Myra stepped in at this point. "You can do lots of different things with sociology, but you would most probably need a second degree, in demography, for example, or criminology, or social work."

"No, I don't really want to do those things," Sarah replied. "I definitely wanted to work in the field of fashion."

"So why study sociology?"

"Because I definitely want to go to university," Sarah insisted. "Furthermore, I took three sociology courses at Clarke and loved them."

"Okay, so go," Myra said.

"But the fashion industry really interests me," Sarah repeated. "I can definitely see myself working in the field."

This discussion went on for a good fifteen minutes, after which Sarah said, "So now do you see why I am so torn."

"Yes, I do," Myra said. "So let me see if I can help you clarify things a little. First, let me say that if you go into fashion right away, your chances of going to university fade a little, since it's a pretty hectic business and you probably would not have time to study sociology once you started working. On the other hand, if you go to university first, you may find yourself chomping at the bit since you are interested in fashion and want to work in the field.

"The bottom line is this—" As she was speaking, Myra finally understood what she should say: "Both fields interest you; you wouldn't be so conflicted if they didn't. So, I think the way I can help you best is by reassuring you that whichever path you choose, you will not be making a mistake."

Sarah was hanging on Myra's every word.

"Yes," Myra repeated. "That's it. You will not be making a mistake no matter which way you go since you can always change your mind and switch."

"That's true," Sarah agreed.

"So that's my advice, or rather my observation. Stop driving yourself crazy. You can't do both, and choosing one now does not mean that you have foreclosed the other. Does that help in any way?" Myra asked.

"Yes, it does. It takes away the pressure of having to decide my entire future now, this very minute. I can always change…Yes." Sarah smiled broadly. "That does help, it helps a lot."

EXCEPT FOR ELIZABETH

Early on in her advising career, Myra noticed that students who wanted to become teachers knew exactly which age group they wanted to work with. For some it was kindergarten, for some upper elementary, for some high school, and for some college, or even university. Rare was the student who knew they wanted to teach but was not sure of the level. Elizabeth knew she wanted to teach but was conflicted about the level.

"Now, that's rare," Myra said. "I haven't been keeping statistics, but I can recall only one case of a student who knew he wanted to teach but was not sure of the level. Almost all students know exactly which age group they want to work with. So why are you conflicted?"

"Well, I'm very creative, and I think that would serve me well if I were to teach kindergarten. But I also love literature, and I know I would love teaching English in high school."

"I see, yes. And the training for early elementary teaching and high school teaching is different. I know it sounds weird, but you can apply to both. Your grades are very good, you will be accepted to both—I checked your record before you came in—and if I may be allowed a personal comment, I just met you but I can tell you're going to be a great teacher—"

"Well, thank you, that's very nice of you."

"Yes, you're calm and composed, you smile readily, I'm sure your students will love you. The only thing is that at some point you are going to have to decide between the two levels. What can I say? I wish you the best whichever you choose."

STOCK-TAKING

Philip and Mrs. Piameng came to see Myra sometime in April. Philip was in his last semester of science and had been doing very well.

"I checked your grades, Philip, congratulations," Myra said. "You must be very proud," Myra said to Mrs. Piameng.

"I am," Mrs. Piameng said. "But—"She shook her head in Philip's direction.

"What seems to be the problem?" Myra asked, turning back to Philip.

"Well," Philip said. "I've been accepted to physical therapy at McGill and I'm no longer sure I want to go."

"Oh," Myra said.

"You see, I've been working very hard to get the grades I got, and all along the idea was to do something in the health field, so I applied to physical therapy..." Philip's voice trailed off.

"So you applied to physical therapy—" Myra repeated Philip's words encouragingly.

"But now that I've been accepted..."

"Now that you've been accepted..."

"It's just more of the same. That's all it is, more of the same."

"I don't understand." Mrs. Piameng addressed Myra. "Physical therapy is such a wonderful field: Philip's future will be secure, he'll be helping people, which is what he wanted." Mrs. Piameng turned to Philip. "That is what you said you wanted, Philip, you said you wanted to help people..."

"Yes, but..."

"So what's going on, Philip?" Myra asked.

"Well, physical therapy is a five-year program, and when you graduate, you go to work...I don't know, it's just more of the same..."

"More of the same what, hard work?"

"Yes. And I already feel it now, I've slacked off this last little while, not enough to be in trouble—" Philip turned to his mother. "Don't worry, Ma, I'm passing and I'll graduate." He turned back to Myra. "But I can feel it; it's not like it was, my heart's just not in it.

"And suddenly, I'm no longer sure about my next step. And that's why we're here, I want to take the year off but my mother doesn't want me to."

"I see."

"I don't understand." Mrs. Piameng looked at Myra. "I just don't understand. This is what he's been working towards all this time and now to want to take off the year…"

"The university will hold his spot. It is possible to defer one's admission, Mrs. Piameng," Myra said.

"But why? In order to travel? That's what Philip wants to do, travel. He can travel after he finishes his studies—"

"I need a break now, Ma," Philip said quietly. "I just can't seem to push myself anymore," Philip addressed Myra. "I just can't seem to do it."

"I think I understand, Philip. I read this somewhere: you need will power to exercise will power."

"Yes, that's it, exactly. The way I see it, there has to be more to life than just studying hard and studying some more and then finding a job and working hard. Not that I want to party for a year; believe me, that's not at all what I want to do. I just feel that I need a break; I want to see what else is out there, see the world a little. I've never done anything but study. I wasn't very active at school, neither here nor in high school. I have friends, but what I've done mostly is study hard—"

"And succeed," Myra pointed out.

Philip managed a wan smile. But then he added quietly, "I know I have to do this."

Myra looked at Mrs. Piameng. "This must be very hard for you—"

"I don't understand what's happening to him, Miss, I just don't understand. To be accepted to physical therapy and to throw it away "

"I'm not throwing it away, Ma. I just need time to think. I need time to breathe…"

STOCK-TAKEN

"And how can I help you on this beautiful spring day?" Myra asked Eleni and her mom, Mrs. Maratos.

"You can help my mother," Eleni said.

"How can I do that?" Myra turned to face Mrs. Maratos.

"You can tell my daughter not to waste her abilities," Mrs. Maratos said. "Have you checked her grades?"

"As a matter of fact, I did; they're beautiful. Congratulations, Eleni."

"Thanks," Eleni said.

"Well, with grades like that she wants to go to esthetician school," Mrs. Maratos said.

"And that's a problem because…?"

"Because with grades like that she could get into law school, she could get into any program she wants at university—"

"But I don't want to be a lawyer, Mom, nor a psychologist nor a teacher." Eleni turned to Myra. "I would have been happy to go to esthetician school right after high school but my mother insisted I go to college. Well, I've gone to college, but now I want to do what I want."

"But she's so bright, she has so much to give—" Mrs. Maratos pleaded with Myra.

"But she wants to be an esthetician," Myra said.

"I can't accept it, I just can't accept it," Mrs. Maratos said.

"Don't you see, Mrs. Maratos, she'll be a fantastic esthetician," Myra said with a smile.

"Is that supposed to make me happy?"

"Well, not exactly happy, but happier?"

"It hurts." Mrs. Maratos pointed to her heart. "It hurts right here. I feel she's wasting her God-given ability."

"I'm curious, Mrs. Maratos, did you think I would agree with you or with your daughter?"

"I don't know what I was thinking."

"It's not just me," Myra added. "All of my colleagues are on the same page about this. How about you, Eleni, what did you think?"

"I was hoping you would agree with me."

"I'm afraid I do agree with your daughter," Myra turned to Mrs. Maratos. "Eleni is mature, she is intelligent, she did not waste her time here, she worked hard, she did beautifully—"

"It's just such a waste," Mrs. Maratos wailed again.

"But if this is what your daughter wants to do…You know, years ago the daughter of a friend of mine left school after a year of CEGEP in order to pursue a career in dancing. She joined a dancing troupe, travelled all over Quebec, she even went overseas a few times. She did this for about five or six years and then she realized she wanted to do something different, and that was when she went back to school. I'm not saying this is what Eleni will do, but you have to let her follow her own path."

Mrs. Maratos remained silent.

"I know you are finding this very difficult, Mrs. Maratos," Myra continued. "But you wouldn't be here if you didn't want the best for Eleni. It's just that your best and her best do not happen to coincide."

Mrs. Maratos did not respond to this either.

"I suppose I was your last hope to try to convince Eleni," Myra added quietly. "But I can't in good conscience try to do that. I just hope your coming here has helped you accept her choice just a little. Maybe, just maybe, I've helped what you know in your mind—". Here, Myra lifted her hand and pointed in the direction of Mrs. Maratos's forehead. "—Move down and help your heart accept this." And Myra lowered her hand slowly to indicate Mrs. Maratos's heart.

"No, the thought is stuck right here." Mrs. Maratos gripped her throat but she did manage a wan smile. "I just find this so hard to accept, so hard." And tears came to her eyes.

"Mrs. Maratos, I'm willing to bet that Eleni will turn out to be an award-winning esthetician, she'll do things with make up that have never been done before. She will be a star in her field…"

ANYTHING BUT

Raffi was a Social Science student who, at one point, decided he wanted to go into kinesiology.

"That takes a science background," Myra explained.

Raffi came back a few weeks later. "What about Occupational Therapy? That's even more along the lines of what I would like to do. I want to work with people in a helping fashion."

"I hate to break it to you, Raffi, but that also takes science. Furthermore, OT is even more competitive than kinesiology, so your science grades would have to be even higher."

Raffi came back just as the semester was coming to an end. "So how long would it take for me to get my science prerequisites done?"

"Well, given that you did not take much science in high school, you would have those courses to make up; that would take a year, and then—"

Raffi's face fell.

"Raffi, why kinesiology, why OT? They are both very honorable professions. But if you want to work with people, and at one point you said you wanted to help youngsters particularly, why not become a teacher—"

"Oh, no, my parents are teachers."

"Oh, I see," Myra said, and she looked Raffi in the eye. "So what you are saying is that you will become anything but, and pass up on a profession for which you easily have the grades to get in, for which you do not need to take high school or college science courses to qualify, a profession in which you would be working with youngsters…"

LOST?

Guido's father had written to Myra as soon as Guido was admitted to Clarke. He wanted some information about how his son could make up for his missing high school mathematics course while at Clarke.

While Guido was attending Clarke, Mr. di Rossi wrote to Myra a second time to get some information about the dates for summer school, since Guido was planning on taking a course then but the family wanted to plan a summer vacation.

Then, just as Guido was about to graduate, Myra received a letter from Mr. di Rossi. It seemed that Guido had no idea what to do after he graduated. *Could you please send me some information about the three-year programs available at CEGEP and the university programs for which Guido is eligible?*

Please have Guido come and see me, Mr. Di Rossi. That would be the most effective way to handle this, Myra wrote back.

Guido did not wait long. He came to see Myra several days later.

Guido's grades were mediocre. He had failed only one course—the math course his father had insisted he take—and from the lowly grade he had received Myra surmised that he had given up on the course and had stopped attending. Otherwise, Guido was a responsible young man who had attended all his other classes and had taken his studies seriously.

"Well, according to your father's letter, you have no idea what to do after you graduate. Is that correct?"

"Pretty much," Guido replied.

"Well, the first thing I recommend is that you take an interest test. This is a service Clarke provides, and since we're getting close to the end of the semester, you have to hurry up if you want to get feedback before the semester is over." Myra reached for an instruction sheet and handed it to Guido. "This is not magic, but it can't hurt. And if it helps, why, that would be wonderful.

"Meanwhile, can I ask you a few questions? Is your father, your mother, an uncle, a friend's father, a neighbor—is anyone you know doing something particularly interesting that you would like to do?"

"No, not really."

"Okay. So let's talk about your program. The three areas that your program has prepared you for—although your grades are not quite strong enough for now—are education, the helping professions, and law. Do any of these appeal to you?"

"Well, the idea of psychology appealed to me, but as you say, my grades are not strong enough and it's too long a haul."

"Social work is also a helping profession; the training for that is not as long as for psychology and it's a little easier to get into." Myra explained further but Guido was not interested, especially when he learned that McGill wanted applicants to have done volunteer work.

"You mean work for free?" Guido asked.

"Yes, but in a social work environment. To see whether the profession interests you."

"No," Guido said. "I do not like that idea at all."

"All right. Have you considered the non-academic fields, the trades? A few years ago a young man came to withdraw from Social Science. His grades were very strong but, as he said, he wanted to work outdoors."

"I don't want to be stuck behind a desk all day either."

"I got the same answer from a young man who was part of a team that did some masonry work on my house a few years ago. He was the only young man on the team, the only one who wore a helmet, who wore steel-toed boots. Clearly he had been to school and had learned about the rules of safety. I asked him what had led him to masonry, and that was his answer, too; he had not wanted to be stuck behind a desk all day, he wanted to work outdoors. So, you're not the only person who thinks that way."

"As a matter of fact, there is one thing that I had thought about—"

"Yes?"

"Enlisting in the army."

"Oh." Myra was as surprised as could be. Guido was a quiet, self-contained young man, introverted—

"So you disapprove, too?"

"Not at all. I—wait a minute, are you saying your parents disapprove?"

"Big time. I've had this idea for a while, and they keep hoping it will go away."

"Well, I can see why they might disapprove, but I can see why it might appeal to you, why it appeals to certain people. It provides structure, but within that structure there are all kinds of possibilities for specialized training."

"Exactly."

"And here I was going on and on about the trades…."

Myra emailed Mr. di Rossi as soon as Guido left. *"Your son is a very fine young man,* she wrote, *and we had a very interesting conversation. But I will leave it to Guido to recount the gist of it."*

Around six months later, Myra received a letter from the Canadian Armed Forces Recruiting Department asking about her interaction with a certain Guido di Rossi…

THE TRADES

The trades do not have a good reputation with most CEGEP students because they are taught in the high schools— specialized centres in the high schools, but high schools, nevertheless. So going there seems like a step down for most CEGEP students, and they fail to explore the great variety of programs available there that just might be the answer to what they are looking for.

Some students find their way on their own, some students need some help.

▶ Petros

Myra feared she had another disappointed potential doctor or engineer on her hands when Petros came to see her because he had failed all his science courses in his first semester at Clarke.

But Petros did not seem particularly perturbed when he sat down. "I know I can retake my science courses, but I don't want to. I came to see you because I want to change into the Social Science program. You see," Petros continued. "I want to be a carpenter. But I'm not in a rush. I want to finish CEGEP and then I'll go to trade school to learn carpentry."

"So how can I help you?" Myra smiled at him, delighted and relieved all at the same time. "It seems to me that you have everything figured out quite nicely."

"I want to know more about Social Science: how to pick my courses, whether any of the courses I did pass can count towards my new program…"

▶ Luis

Luis was even more forthright than Petros. When he sat down in front of Myra, the first thing he said was that he was a barber.

"A barber?" Myra queried.

"Yes, a barber. I taught myself by going on YouTube. Then I began to cut my friends' hair. They paid me for it, and then I went to this barber shop near my house, have you heard of it, HairKuts?"

"Sorry, no, I haven't."

"It's quite pricey, and I watched the fellow who cut my hair and I watched the other barbers. I kept doing this, cutting the hair of my friends, using the money to go to HairKuts and learning as much as I could. I got to know the owner and we began talking, and he took me on for a trial period. Then he offered me a job because he said I was good with the clients. They even began to ask for me. Now I work there on Fridays and Saturdays. So, you see, I'm a barber."

"That's pretty fantastic. So how can I help you?"

"I want to learn more about business. I want to transfer into Clarke's business program so that if I ever want to open my own shop…"

A few weeks later, Myra came across a news feed item that an Ontario barber was suing the Ontario government for not offering an apprenticeship program for barbers, that barbering was not recognized as a trade. Hairstyling was, and hairstylists could join the Ontario College of Trades, but barbers could not. Hmm, Myra thought, she would never have stopped to read this item if not for Luis.

Luis helped Myra in another way. Before, whenever students told her they wanted to work with people, teaching, psychology, or management came to mind, but now she added barbering and hairstyling to the list. For didn't she adore her hairstylist and always have very interesting exchanges with her?

Myra's hairstylist agreed. She had had a client a few days earlier who was going through a very rough patch, and she felt as if she had just been the client's therapist for the half-hour it took to cut and style her hair.

Several weeks later Myra saw another news feed that took things to an even higher level. It seemed that Black barbers in LA were being enlisted to help alert their Black clientele to the dangers of high blood pressure, Black men being at higher risk for hypertension than white men. And the idea was being applied to women, too, with hair stylists being trained to recognize and make referrals for clients who showed signs of being victims of domestic violence.

▶ Sally

Sally had not done well at the first college she had attended, and had changed to Clarke hoping things would go better there. Well, she was not doing much better at Clarke than at her first college. "What was it you said you wanted to be, a history teacher?" Myra asked after Sally had sat down.

"Yes, it's one of the few subjects I liked in high school and that I like in the program I'm in."

"So, you like to read?"

"No, why do you ask?"

"Well, if you want to study history, you're going to have to do a lot of reading.

"And writing, too, come to think of it," Myra added a moment later.

Sally's face fell.

"Well, if you don't like to read, what is it you do like?" Myra asked.

"I love shopping."

"Have you considered a career in retailing?" Myra asked and proceeded to give Sally names of schools to contact.

▶ Marlene

Myra could not help noticing that Marlene had the most beautiful nails,

But Marlene was stymied. This was her first semester at Clarke and she was not doing well in her courses. She could not explain it. She enjoyed the atmosphere, she enjoyed her friends, but she was not enjoying her classes, and worst of all, she couldn't get herself to do the readings. "I was always a pretty serious student and I did all right in high school, but CEGEP is just not working for me."

"Do you have any idea about what you want to do?"

"No, that's the trouble, I don't."

"Well, the first thing I noticed about you was that your nails are gorgeous. Did you do them yourself?"

"Yes, I did."

"Well, have you ever thought about a career in something having to do with that? There's a whole world out there that isn't academic, that isn't CEGEP, something that might interest you and will use your natural skills—aesthetics, hairdressing, pedicurist, laser hair removal."

Marlene's face relaxed a little. "No, I never did."

"Well, here are some telephone numbers…"

HISTORY

▶ Pablo

It was none of her business, but Myra was curious. The twinning of the surname Pablo with the family name Grossman was unusual.

After having answered Pablo's questions about his forthcoming application to university, Myra finally did ask him about it.

"Oh, my father is Jewish," Pablo explained. "Although my mother isn't. I wasn't raised Jewish, but my father is, and of course, his parents are.

"It's quite the story. My grandfather was born in Austria but managed to escape the country with his wife right after the Nazis took over. He had a good friend in Mexico, so that's why they ended up in Mexico."

"I was lucky," Myra said. "I was born here. But except for my mother and one of her brothers, my mother's entire family was wiped out. And as young as I was at the time, I could tell from the way my mother was worried, that something very bad was happening somewhere far away, something very, very bad.

"Is your grandfather still alive?" Myra brought the conversation back to Pablo.

"Yes."

"Does he live here or in Mexico?"

"He lives in Mexico. He said he was too old to change countries at his age."

"But your family goes home to visit, right? You should ask him about it, Pablo. You're interested in history, you have living history right there in your household."

▶ Jonathan

When Myra came across the name Jonathan Thessalonikios she did a double-take. Of course, the name was Greek, but when she sounded it out, she saw that the name was the name of the city she knew as Salonika. And Salonika was a city, which, during WWII, had had almost its entire Jewish population rounded up and exterminated three days after the Germans marched in. It was a name that had always given her the shivers—she imagined her Greek brethren standing at the kitchen sink washing vegetables and, suddenly, hearing a pounding at the door with that blood-curdling shout: "*Raus…*"

Three days, that's all it had taken the Germans to clear the city of its Jewish population, three days!

So, Thessalonikios.

As for the first name, she had never seen a Greek student with the name Jonathan. And there were lots of Greek students at Clarke. So after having answered Jonathan's question about his course selection, Myra asked him about his interesting family name.

And, sure enough, Jonathan's grandfather had changed their family name to Thessalonikios to sound more Greek, and yes, they were Jewish and had managed to evade the roundups. He didn't know the whole story, but—

And Myra had interrupted him. "Get the story while you can, Jonathan, like right away. Not for my sake, for your sake, get the story from your grandfather."

I'M NOT MOTIVATED

If asked, Myra would admit to a bias against students who did not listen, the kinds of students who ask a question and who, while you are answering their question, ask another, and then another, and so on. There was something about how these young people were wired, that they had to jump from moment to moment and could not let the moment come to them.

But if these young people were so wired, why be annoyed? But, of course, they were at the same time involuntarily—it did present itself as involuntary—not paying heed to the information she was trying to give them. No wonder this type of student did not do well, Myra thought

But one week in late fall, when the semester was drawing to a close, Myra had two students come to her within the space of a few days with a new kind of complaint, one she had not heard before, or, certainly, had not heard expressed in exactly that way: two students who made the hot-wired students seem refreshing.

▶ Drew

Drew was failing his courses. But he didn't seem particularly upset by this. "I'm not motivated," he said.

Myra tried to keep her expression neutral. Drew's words, tone and, above all, his limp, sagging posture conveyed the belief that he had explained himself, that he saw himself as suffering from a disease that had felled him, a condition that exonerated him from all effort and explained his situation.

"Well, what made you go into the program you are in?" Myra asked.

"I thought I would like it."

"And you don't?"

"Not at all."

"Have you been working on your General Education courses?"

"No."

"Have you been going to class at all?"

"No."

"Okay, so how can I help you? You must have had a reason for coming to see an academic advisor other than to tell me you are not motivated?"

"One of my friends told me to come."

"I see. Well I can tell you what's going to happen, but from your tone, from your demeanor, I get the impression you do not intend to come back to Clarke."

"No, I don't."

"On the chance that someday you might, I'll just tell you that you are going to get a letter from the College informing you that you are in bad academic standing. This letter will also inform you of the procedures you have to follow to be allowed to return. Should you change your mind and decide to come back in a year or two, having signed the letter will make you eligible to do so."

"Okay."

"So what do you plan to do?"

"I'm going to Audio College. I want to learn to write songs and they teach that there."

"They do? I thought they teach audio engineering."

"No, my friend told me they teach song   writing."

"Have you called them? Did you ask? You had better check this out. Just a minute." Myra turned to her computer and pulled up Audio College. She read through the site info quickly. "Drew, you had better check this out. They don't say anything about song writing on their website."

"That's all right, Miss, I know what I'm doing."

"Drew, do yourself a favour and call them. They have pretty steep tuition fees…"

▶ Patricia

A few days later it was Patricia's turn to utter those fateful words, "I'm not motivated," with the same lack of tone, the same passiveness, the same sagging posture as Drew's.

She was right, Myra thought, there was a new virus out there, a new disease that was ravaging young people, a mysterious flu that was laying them low and leaving them powerless.

"I have no idea why I'm here," Patricia elaborated.

"Here in this office, or here at Clarke?" Myra asked.

"Both, I guess."

"Let's start with Clarke, you're the one who applied to come here—"

"No, my parents were the ones who insisted I go to college."

"I see."

"I did try at the beginning, I did go to class, but, honestly, Miss, it's not for me."

"So why didn't you withdraw?"

"Withdraw?"

"Yes, withdraw, officially delete your courses and inform the college you no longer wanted to be here. Now you're going to get failures in everything."

"Oh."

"It doesn't bother you?"

"Not particularly."

"I see. Okay, now what about my office, do you have any idea why you're here?"

"Well, a friend of mine told me to come and see someone."

"If you give me an idea of what you like, what you might want to do, I might be able to help."

"I haven't the faintest idea."

"Do you work?"

"Yes."

"Do you like your job?"

"Not particularly."

"But you didn't stop attending your job?"

"Of course, not." Patricia looked at Myra quizzically. Was Myra pulling her leg? She wouldn't stop attending her job.

"Well, Patricia, since you're still officially an attending student and there is still time, I suggest you do an interest test and attend a career workshop. It's not magic, it's not going to tell you what to do so that you will become rich and famous and live happily ever after, but it might give you a few ideas…"

MATURITY

On the opposite end of the pole, there was Elwood.

Tall and good-looking, Elwood had come to verify something about his course selection for his forthcoming last semester when he would be graduating.

All was in order, and Myra asked him what his plans were after graduating.

"Oh, I want to go into business. I want to do well. Not that I think money is the be-all and end-all, but I'm not ashamed to say it, I want the good life."

"So did you have a job while attending Clarke?" Myra asked.

"Yes. Here and there. For example, this weekend I helped out downtown, during the condominium sale near the Bell Centre. I was just clerking, but watching the people put down their fifty-

and one hundred-thousand dollar down payments, you have to wonder, where do people get this kind of money? I don't know whether I'll ever make it like that, but I sure am going to give it a try.

"On the other hand," Elwood continued. "My mother is an art teacher and she loves what she does. I have no intention of forgetting that there's that in my background as well."

POSTURE

Myra had been giving Nikki bad news from the moment she met her.

Nikki had been admitted to Clarke two years before and had failed all her courses miserably. Now she was back, trying very hard to get back into day studies, but she had to upgrade her academic record by passing four evening courses before being readmitted to full-time studies during the day.

The first piece of bad news Myra delivered to Nikki when she met her was that her dream of getting into law school straight from college was probably just that, now, a dream, since her record during the two semesters when she had registered and not attended was so bad, her overall cumulative average would probably never be high enough to make it into law.

Now Nikki was in the process of taking three evening classes and she had come to see Myra to try to get into a January intersession course—a course scheduled to start and finish before regular classes started in late January—to add the fourth course she was missing and hopefully start day classes in the winter.

Normally, evening students did not have access to those intersession courses, but there happened to be room in the course that Nikki wanted and Myra was able to get her into it.

Now Nikki had come to find out when she could register for day classes.

"But you're not eligible to start day classes in January," Myra explained. "The course you are taking is a January course. Even though it finishes before the regular semester starts, it's a January course."

Nikki stared at Myra blankly.

Had she not made this clear to Nikki when she first came to see her, Myra asked herself, and her heart sank. And then she remembered Nikki had come to see her on the recommendation of one of Clarke's counsellors. He was the one who had thought the intersession course might qualify Nikki for day studies, and Myra could not remember whether she had ever disabused Nikki of this idea.

Myra tried to explain. "If a Clarke student admitted to university for the winter fails a course in the fall and passes that course during the January intersession period, he or she still does not qualify for admission to university. The January intersession course is part of the winter semester. The fact that it finishes before regular winter classes start does not change that fact."

Nikki continued to stare at Myra blankly.

"Or, to put it another way, the student who takes his or her last course during the January intersession period graduates in June, not in December."

Nikki's whole body slumped forward, as if collapsing in on itself.

"I'm sorry, Nikki, those are the rules."

But then Nikki thought of something. She unfolded herself from her chair as she raised her head, straightened her shoulders, and sat up very straight. "Even if I do very well in the intersession course?" she argued.

"Even if you do very well in your course. You're not eligible, the admissions office will not wait for the results.

Nikki's head drooped forward again, as did her shoulders, and she slumped back down in her chair.

"I know you must be disappointed," Myra said. "But you have one more semester to go before you can be admitted to full-time day studies." Myra turned to look at Nikki's latest results on her computer screen. "I must say, though, your grades this past semester are not just good, they're spectacular."

Nikki pulled herself up tall and straight again. She had found another argument. "What if my grade in the January course is just as spectacular?"

Myra shook her head. "I just explained, the admissions office will not wait for those results."

Whatever had given Nikki the strength to sit up straight left her, and she burrowed down in her chair again.

"Look, Nikki, I'm sorry I never made this perfectly clear to you in the past, but you have one more semester of evening studies before you can be admitted to day studies."

Nikki pulled herself up slowly. "I understand. Thank you for all you did for me." She got up and left Myra's office.

A day or two later Myra remembered how she could legally circumvent the rules and grant Nikki's wish. She had it in her power to allow an evening student to take day classes, if there was room in the day classes. It did not change the status of the student, they remained an evening student and, in Nikki's case, were still not allowed to register for full-time studies, but...

Why had she not thought of this while Nikki was in her office?

Myra knew why: because the counsellor who had brought Nikki to her had prejudiced her against Nikki. He did not think Nikki had been frank with him and he had voiced his reservations to Myra. Nikki had hidden the fact that she was no longer in full-time studies from her very authoritarian, tradition-bound parents—how had she managed to do this, what else was she not telling them, he had wondered. And Myra had been influenced by his misgivings.

So what had changed, Myra asked herself. For one, there was Nikki's dignity when she had delivered the bad news to her about day studies. And two, Nikki's grades, which really were spectacular. She was a sucker for good grades, Myra admitted readily.

In reply to Myra's email informing Nikki of the possibility of taking two courses in the day division, Nikki wrote: *Happy Holidays to you, too. I wish you a wonderful new year filled with abundance, joy, and treasured moments. May the coming year be your best year yet!*

Thank you a couple of thousand times.

The girl has talent, Myra thought.

And after all these years, Myra added as an aside to herself, she still had to remember to take people on their own terms and not on terms defined by, and unfortunately often deformed by, others.

DIFFERENT FOLKS

▶Tasneem

Tasneem was a serious student who came to see Myra several times about her program and the sequencing of her courses.

One summer, Tasneem registered for a biology course. But a day after the delete deadline, she called Myra in a panic. Suddenly, her family was going on a trip and she had to drop the course. She had spoken to the person in charge and was told it was not possible to drop the course. Was there anything Myra could do?

No, Myra replied, she did not have the authority to do anything. However, the Registrar did. His name was Jim. Call this number—Myra gave Tasneem the secretary's number—and ask to see Jim.

Two days later Tasneem showed up in Myra's office with a gift. "Thank you, thank you so much. I saw the Registrar yesterday and he allowed me to delete the course. I don't know how to thank you. So I brought you this."

"It wasn't necessary," Myra said. Myra and Tasneem chatted a little while longer, then Tasneem left.

Myra opened the little package. It was a gift card from her favourite shopping centre that could be used in any of the stores there. When she turned the gift card over, she gasped. It was for the sum of one hundred dollars. Her elation disappeared. She could not accept such a large sum of money from a student. Advisors occasionally received chocolate or a bottle of wine from a grateful student, but one hundred dollars…

The next morning Myra wrote a polite but firm letter to Tasneem.

Thank you for your generous gift.
I must say, though, when I saw the amount, I was taken aback. I know you and your parents meant well, but I can't possibly accept it. Please come and take it back. I will not be using it, so if you do not come back, it will be as if you were throwing out a hundred dollars.
I just want to add, I didn't do anything. All I did was tell you the person to speak to who did have the authority to help. I am glad things worked out for you.
Since you insist on thanking me in a practical way, however, I will tell you that students do sometimes thank us with chocolate or a bottle of wine. And since I love chocolate, I will tell you I love Lindt Madagascar 70% and Lindt Sea Salt chocolate bars.
Please come and take the gift card back.

Tasneem called immediately. No, her father insisted. It was part of their culture to show appreciation in this manner.

Yes, Myra replied, she knew that, and she appreciated the gesture, but it was part of her culture not to accept this kind of gift. She insisted, Tasneem had to come and retrieve the gift card. As she had written, not to do so would be like tearing up one hundred dollars.

Tasneem came by later that morning with Myra's favourite chocolate but with two bars of each rather than one.

"Thank you, Tasneem. And thank your father," Myra said. "And good luck."

▶ Sadat

Sadat was in the third year of his business program and had just become engaged to get married. The problem was that his fiancée lived in Ohio and he would be moving there before he finished his program. Was it possible to finish his studies in Columbus?

"You would have to find a college there with a business program and ask to have the courses you took credited there. The receiving institution decides, we don't. Keep all your course outlines. That's the kind of documentation they will want in order to be able to evaluate the work you did here. It's called asking for equivalences.

"The only way I can help is to give you a letter that explains our system of education. Let me know when you want the letter and I'll prepare it for you."

Sadat came back a second time to ask whether he could finish his program at Clarke sooner. He had heard there were intersession courses, could he take those?

No, his program courses were not offered in that format. He had a full year to do, there was no compressing all those courses into less time.

The third time Sadat came back, he asked about online courses. Maybe he could do a few of those in the summer and get ahead?

Clarke did not have any online courses. There was a CEGEP that offered online business courses, but those courses were offered only in French, and his French was not strong enough.

When Sadat came back a fourth time, Myra laughed. "I give you points for trying, but, honestly, if there were a way, I would tell you."

But this time Sadat had come back to ask whether Myra would be interested in coming to his wedding.

"My goodness, that's very nice of you. But I would feel very lost. I wouldn't know anybody. But thanks, that's very sweet."

"Yes, I told my parents how helpful you have been, and they suggested it."

"Thank your parents for me. It certainly would have been an interesting experience."

Myra and Sadat continued to chat, especially about how different their backgrounds were, hers North-American and Jewish, his Pakistani and Moslem.

And because the subject was still fresh in everyone's mind, the subject of 9/11 came up.

After a few preliminary comments, Sadat voiced his skepticism about the identity of the culprits. "The whole thing was a plot to malign Moslems," he said. "Everyone knows who did it." Being a polite young man, he said no more, but looked at Myra meaningfully.

Oh, my god, Myra thought, she had a live one right in front of her. A living, breathing purveyor of the old poison bottled and remarketed to a huge, new, and very willing audience.

Myra brought their conversation to a quick end. Thankfully, Sadat did not come back to see her.

▶ Ali

Ali was a middle-aged man who had taken an Attestation in Business in Clarke's evening division and had transferred to the day division in order to get his Diploma in Business, a longer, more substantial version of his former program.

Planning when Ali was to take all the courses he was missing—some courses were offered only in the fall, some only in the winter—took some doing, but Myra worked it out with him. After that, she became his go-to person for all kinds of situations.

One time, Ali needed to change a late afternoon course for an earlier section to accommodate his work.

Another time, Ali asked to take a course in the evening. This, too, had been for work purposes, because during that particular semester he needed an entire day free during the week for his job.

A third time, Ali asked for a schedule change because his Friday noon class was conflicting with his religious obligations.

One day, Ali came to talk to Myra about going to university. Myra gave Ali the information he was seeking and then asked how his courses were going.

"They are going well. I am learning a lot," Ali said.

"I'm glad. I'd be upset if you told me you were wasting your time."

"Oh, I meant I'm learning more than just business things."

"You are? Like what?"

"Well, last semester I took this Leadership course and it changed me. I used to be very bossy with my children; after all, I'm their father, I know what's best. But in this course we learned about different styles of leadership and I decided to try it out on my children, especially my two older boys. They were becoming quite difficult, and I thought, what do I have to lose? Well, guess what, it works, it really works."

"Ali, did you tell your teacher? You have to tell your teacher. Have you any idea how pleased he would be? You absolutely have to tell him."

▶ Viktor

Viktor was not happy. He had come to complain about his English and Humanities teachers.

He was having major trouble in their classes because he did not share their outlook on life, their political views, their points of view.

It took Myra a moment to understand. "Their political views, their points of view, meaning—"

"Meaning that if you don't agree with them, they give you a really hard time. I thought English was about presenting your point of view grammatically and coherently, not about what it is you are saying. The same goes for Humanities.

"At first I thought I may have misunderstood the teacher's instructions, but it's been like that in all the English and Humanities courses I've taken so far."

"And these courses were—" Myra called up the information on her computer. "Crime and Prejudice, Challenging the Obvious, Media, Myth and Propaganda—"

"My point of view is different from that of most people," Viktor said. "It's certainly different from that of my teachers. I don't believe in socialism, which is what we have today. I don't believe in the welfare state, I don't believe that all people are equal, I don't believe that men and women are equal—"

"If by equal you mean the same, I would agree with you. If you mean that one sex is superior to the other—"

"Men are stronger than women for a reason, Miss, just like white people have accomplished things that Blacks and Indians have not. I can go on and on. And the result of all this is the weakening of morals, the weakening of society, an everything-goes attitude. Well, I believe in discipline, I believe in physical strength, and, yes, I believe in the superiority of white people. This is radically different from what most people think, but people have been wrong before; what's popular has been wrong before, popular does not mean that it's right."

"Do you live at home, Viktor, do your parents share your views?"

"No, I don't, I moved out because I wanted to be on my own. I don't get along with either of my parents, but the point is, if we are all supposed to be equal, which is what the other side says, how come what I say is not allowed, how come what I say is being squelched?"

"You are being judged on the content of what you are saying and not the quality, is that it?"

"That's exactly it."

"Well, I would say, on the basis of our brief conversation so far, your ability to express yourself is definitely superior to that of most of the students I deal with."

"Thank you. Look, I know what people think, I know what my contemporaries think when they think. I know I'm in the minority, but that's not a reason not to grade me fairly."

"Yes. But if I may be permitted, if I were your teacher and you said offensive things about women, I might find it difficult to separate the two."

"I never said offensive things about women, I just said men are stronger, that men are being put down in present society, that men are born to lead, that the whole drift of society is anti-male, anti-white male in particular, that the time has come to change this. And there are others out there who agree with me, who are beginning to wake up, to organize..."

Myra called Jean-Francois Roussel as soon as Viktor left her office. Viktor was in Jean-Francois' program and she needed to talk to someone about him. Viktor did not seem angry, but the things he said about others out there waking up and organizing could lead to major trouble.

It turned out that Jean-Francois had already had many long conversations with Viktor, that he was continuing to reach out to him and engage with him. "Let's keep in touch, Myra. If Viktor comes back to see you, let me know. I think he is salvageable. He's not a die-hard fascist. I think he is very lost and trying to find his way."

Several months later Jean-Francois dropped by Myra's office. He had come to give her an update on Viktor's activities. Viktor had indeed become involved with some very dangerous, very violent people, and as their plotting became more and more serious and their actions more and more imminent, he had pulled back. He had even volunteered to share what he knew with the authorities in the hope of neutralizing the group and pulling it down. The information he volunteered had turned out to be quite valuable.

"It could have gone the other way, too, I guess," Myra said.

"Yes," Jean-Francois agreed. "But as we both saw, Viktor was not an angry young man; his was more an intellectual search, and he had gotten mixed up with some very dangerous people. His native decency did not allow him to go all the way, thank goodness. I've encouraged him to stay in touch. I hope he finds his way."

▶ Omar

Omar's problem was that he was in four courses but that he could not continue in one of them for religious reasons. But if he failed this course, he would be in bad standing a second time, because he had failed one of his four courses the previous semester, which meant he would have to leave day studies…

"One thing at a time, Omar," Myra said. "Why can't you continue in one of your present courses?"

"It's a photography course, and I'm not allowed to take photos of humans and animals."

"So why did you register for this course if you knew that?"

"Nothing else fit my schedule, and I thought I'd be able to photograph what I wanted, but it seems I have to include some photos of people to fulfill the course's requirements."

"And you learned about these requirement when?"

"Just now."

"I don't think so. You received a course outline the first day of class; the requirements would have been listed there. That would have been the time to change courses. We're into the fourth week of class now, it's way too late—"

"I was unable to attend the first few days of school—"

Myra looked up at Omar but did not say anything.

"And the course I failed last term, that wasn't my fault, either. The teacher did not mark one of my papers because she said it was handed in late," Omar complained.

"It was handed in late?"

"Well, I was busy, and I thought a few days wouldn't make a difference; she never said—"

"That course also had an outline, so the policy on late assignments would have been spelled out in the outline. Let's take a look, shall we?" Myra turned to her computer, did a little navigating, and found the course outline in question. She read through it quickly. When she got to the relevant paragraph she turned the monitor in Omar's direction. "Here, take a look at this."

"….late papers will be accepted only if I am notified in advance and only if submitted within three school days of the original deadline."

"I never saw that. I don't think I ever got one of those either," Omar said.

"Did you miss the first few days of class last semester as well?"

"Look, I have things to do other than school—"

"No one said you couldn't do those other things, Omar, but Clarke has a few rules, rules that aren't even that strict, but you are breaking all of them."

"Are you saying I can't change the photography class now?"

"That's correct, it's too late to change courses now. You can drop your course but you can't add another course at this point, after three full weeks of school. So the answer is no."

Omar stared at Myra coldly.

"There is one thing you can do. You can drop the photography course, but that would make you a part-time student, in which case you would have to pay for your remaining courses. Let's see, that would cost you—" Myra did the calculations quickly. "About two hundred dollars."

"I don't have that kind of money. Besides, I'm on student loans and bursaries."

"Right, and if you became a part-time student, you would no longer qualify for a student loan."

"That's why you have to change my course for me."

"I already told you, the answer is no."

"Is there anyone else I can speak to?"

"Yes, the Registrar."

"I want to see him."

"Fine. Let me see whether he's free now." Myra called over. "Yes, he's in, he'll see you now. You'll find him in Room B-202."

Omar turned away from Myra brusquely, got up, and left her office without saying another word.

The feeling is mutual, Myra thought, as she turned to the paperwork she had been busy with before Omar arrived and picked up where she had left off.

PERFECTIONIST

Myra had heard about Lorraine from a colleague. Lorraine was a woman in her late forties who had attended Clarke years ago and had performed brilliantly, except she had not completed her studies at the time. Lorraine was redoing some science courses in order to qualify for admission to Clarke's Nursing program. Lorraine's abilities had not left her and her request was granted.

Three weeks after classes started, Lorraine came to Myra to withdraw from her program. She held it together for the first few minutes and then started to cry.

She had been hospitalized for anorexia when she was younger, which was why she had not completed her studies many years ago, Lorraine explained. She had come to withdraw because she knew herself, she had begun to feel the same symptoms she had felt years ago when she had been anorexic. And Lorraine pointed to her chest. "There's a tightness here that will not let go, a type of anxiety that I recognized immediately."

"Well, then, you're making the right decision," Myra said.

"You know," Lorraine continued. "I've been working for this all these years, I've saved enough so I don't have to work while I'm in school, I planned it all, and now…

"I don't know how the others do it. There are single moms in the program, there are working moms in the program, there are younger students who live on their own but who also have to work…

"I'm not blaming anyone, but the teachers don't stop putting on the pressure. The first thing they said to us was that half of us won't make it to graduation, that the workload is immense, that…

"I know myself. I recognised my symptoms right away. And my brother, who looks out for me, picked up on it, too. 'Are you sure you're all right?' he asked me when he called me a few nights ago."

"If it's any consolation to you," Myra said. "I have another name for the Nursing program. Nursing sounds so innocuous. 'I think I'll go into Nursing,' people say, as if they're about to go get themselves a cup of coffee. But about two years ago, after three relatively decent students came to see me early one winter day because they had all failed the first semester of Nursing, I started calling the program by another name, mini-medicine."

Lorraine smiled through her tears. "That's definitely more like it. And I don't know how the young students do it either," Lorraine continued. "I heard a second-year student tell a classmate of mine, 'you can't have a life while you're in this program, you have to study all the time'.

"And the faculty does not let us forget it either, not for a minute." Lorraine started to cry again. "I can't do it. I thought I could, I thought I was ready, but I can't do it."

"Lorraine," Myra said. "You know yourself. This is not a failure, this is a health issue. You have the brainpower, that's for sure, look at your grades—" Myra swivelled her computer monitor in Lorraine's direction. "But if the effort it requires from you is going to make you a nervous wreck, and you are wise enough to recognize the symptoms before they do, why then, all I can say is that you are doing the right thing."

"I've been planning this for years. I have a great job, my boss loves me—I hope he'll take me back—"

"I would," Myra said.

Lorraine smiled. "Thank you for being so understanding. I was hesitant to come but I really had no choice."

Myra filled out the withdrawal card and handed it to Lorraine to sign. "Let me know what happens with your job. For what it's worth, I think you would have made a great nurse. But if there's something about this profession that makes you so anxious, well, then, it's not the profession for you."

"Thank you," Lorraine said. "Thank you very much."

Several months later Myra learned from her colleague that Lorraine had been doing well in Nursing, that she had gotten high eighties in the two quizzes she had had, the highest grades in the class. But, of course, nothing less than perfect scores had been acceptable….

SCARRED

～～～

The thing Myra found hardest about her job was hearing the complaints students had about their teachers and not being able to do anything about it.

For the rude and demeaning ones, there was nothing to be said. They did not belong in teaching and were a disgrace to the profession.

For the arrogant ones who liked to show up students by setting killer exams, she had contempt.

For the nice but hopeless pedagogues, of which, unfortunately, there were also a few, she wished mightily they had chosen another profession.

As for the ones who terrorized students with their unreasonable demands, she wished the tables could be turned on these closet sadists.

Camille was a Nursing student who had had to work hard to get into the program, and had had to work even harder to succeed in the program. She was about to start her last semester when she took an intersession course with Teacher X.

"So how did it go?" Myra asked when Camille came by to discuss her application to university.

Myra and Camille had become good friends, so Camille blurted it right out. "She's crazy," she said. "Crazy. You forget to capitalize a word, zero. You don't format your answer the way she told you to, zero. 'I'm preparing you for university,' she says. I don't believe it for a minute. Look, Miss, Nursing is tough, really tough. There is a ton of material to learn, then you have to apply it, plus you're always being observed so you always have to be on. But that's okay, it's part of the learning process. But it's also the nature of the work, the seriousness of what you're doing and the importance of getting it right. But this—I tell you, she's crazy."

"How about the rest of the students in the class?"

"We all stayed in, we were all in the same situation. We needed the course to graduate, so we stayed in. But I'm in my sixth semester of Nursing, I've done five clinical rotations, I've survived them all, but this—this—I'm scarred, I tell you, scarred."

TIME'S UP

Ivor Grande must have been in his late twenties. He was well-spoken and seemed to have some successful business experience behind him given the cut of his suit and the quality of his shirt and tie.

Well, Ivor Grande wanted to take CEGEP-level science courses without ever having taken science courses in high school.

He was not taking no for an answer. And the trouble was that Eileen, new to the Advising Department, was sitting in on the interview as part of her training.

"But what if I know I can do it?" Ivor said yet again.

"How can you say that," Myra said. "Never having taken any chemistry and physics courses before? Would you insist on registering in Spanish IV never having taken Levels I, II, and III Spanish?"

"But I don't want to take Spanish courses, I want to take science courses."

"Mr. Grande, you are not hearing what I am saying."

"No," Ivor Grande replied. "You are not hearing what I am saying. I don't have time to waste taking remedial chemistry and physics courses."

"These courses are called remedial because they are remedying the absence of readiness on the part of a student to absorb CEGEP-level science material," Myra said, for the third time she was pretty sure. "We are not a high school, Mr. Grande," she continued, also for the third time. "Clarke is a college, and the science taught here is college-level science, for which the preparation is high school science. Because we get lots of students who come from high school without any background in high school science, we and many other CEGEPs offer high school-level courses for anyone, including an adult like you, who decides to change direction and go into science. Mathematics must be included because you cannot do physics without math, just like you can't do chemistry at CEGEP without first having taken chemistry in high school."

"How about if I register for the courses I need, and if I can't handle them, I drop the course I am having trouble with?"

"First, the registration system would not allow it unless I overrode it, which I am not prepared to do. And were I to override the system and my supervisor to find out, not only would she be mightily disappointed in me, she would have grounds to discipline me."

"What if I took just two CEGEP courses instead of three—"

"Mr. Grande, we're going around in circles."

"But you don't understand. I have been thinking about this, and finally decided I want to do it, that I am ready. I have done some reading on my own and I feel I am ready."

I wonder what Eileen thinks of all of this, Myra thought. Because she, Myra, was wondering how she was going to get this man out of her office. He was clearly prepared to sit there all morning repeating himself while everything she was saying bounced right off him. Well, he had already taken up more time than he was entitled to. Suddenly, she knew. Yes, and she stood up. "I'm very sorry, Mr. Grande," she announced. "This interview is over." She looked Mr. Grande in the eye. "I am afraid I cannot help you. If I thought there was a way I would certainly tell you what it was. But there is no way, and I am afraid I have to say that this interview is now at an end."

Mr. Grande got up reluctantly. Myra controlled herself and said nothing. If she offered a word of sympathy, she would never get him to leave. She continued looking at him silently. He got the message, turned, and left her office.

OH, DEAR

► Mr. Erdem

Mr. Erdem had been a high-ranking hotel executive in Istanbul but had run afoul of the hotel's president. He had come to Montreal to make a fresh start and wished to acquire local credentials to help him with his job search.

With the help of a very willing teacher in Clarke's Continuing Education Department, Myra was able to put together a package of courses for Mr. Erdem that he could complete in two semesters instead of the normal four. But doing so necessitated a lot of telephoning back and forth. Once, when Myra called Mr. Erdem, she reached his voicemail and heard this message: "Hi, you have reached Mehmet Erdem. I am not home right now. Please leave your message and I will get you back."

▶ Thanh

Thanh was not doing well in Calculus, partly because his English was so poor. He spoke Vietnamese at home, had gone to French school where he had not spoken much English, and had come to Clarke primarily to improve his English. He had not known the words in English for plane, for slope, etc., and had fallen behind in Calculus from the beginning and had never been able to catch up. "How do you say it, I was scre—I was screwed," he said triumphantly, as he looked at Myra with a smile.

Myra could not help smiling in return. "Uh, Thanh, I understand exactly what you mean, but I have to tell you…"

HAIRCUT

Before Brandon came into her office, Myra checked his academic record on her computer. Brandon was close to graduating and he had done well in his courses. When Brandon came into her office, she saw a tall, well-groomed young man who had clearly just had a haircut.

"I just looked up your file and saw your ID photo. Your hair was a little longer when you started Clarke," Myra said.

"You should have seen it before I had this haircut," Brandon said.

"That must have made your mother very happy," Myra commented.

Brandon's face froze. "How did you—when did you—wait, do you know my mother?"

Myra could not help laughing. "No, I do not," she reassured him. "But I'm a mother, and my son also let his hair grow when he was a teenager."

KINDRED SPIRIT

The principal instrument Clarke's music students studied at the College was written on their computer profile. So when Ronald called with a potential registration problem he feared he might encounter in the coming winter semester, his last semester, Myra saw that he was a jazz trumpeter and commented briefly about this.

Ronald assented, yes, he was a jazz trumpeter, but, he added, this did not mean that he didn't love classical music. For example, his favourite piece of music was Rachmaninoff's *Second Piano Concerto*. It made him cry every time he listened to it.

Really, Myra exclaimed, it was one of her favourites, too. He had to try to find the film, Brief Encounter.

No, he hadn't.

"It's an old film, made in the mid 1940's, no frills, black and white, but the Rachmaninoff piano concerto is the background music to the film and is perfectly adapted to the story, a heart-breaking love story." She would send him the reference. He had to promise to try to find the film.

Myra made it a point to contact Ronald during the winter semester. No, he had been too busy, but he hadn't forgotten.

Later, Myra was sorry she hadn't thought of it at the time, and sent Ronald a copy of the film. She had so badly wanted to share it with him.

THINKING AHEAD

Deshawn wanted to get into law school, but his grades were not at law-school level.

Myra's heart sank.

But then she asked him why he wanted to become a lawyer.

Because he wanted to become a sports agent.

And Myra's heart lightened considerably. She knew you did not have to be a lawyer to become a sports agent.

But then Deshawn went on to describe what he had been up to. He had contacted various sports agency companies and groupings in the States to ask whether they had any internship programs and whether they had a spot for him this coming summer. He didn't care if they didn't pay, he wanted the experience.

Myra took a closer look at this young man. Suddenly, her heart felt even lighter. She was looking at someone who was not waiting for things to happen but someone who would do whatever he could to make things happen.

"Good for you, Deshawn. I have to tell you, you already know more about this than I do. If you succeed in connecting with anyone this summer please let me know. And, for sure, the next time I deal with a student wanting to become a sports agent, I'll tell him about what I just learned from you."

GUARDIAN ANGELS

▶ Costa

Costa came back to Clarke to finish the program he had started years ago. He came to see Myra to make sure he registered for the right courses and to ensure that he took them in the right sequence.

"My goodness, your first sojourn at Clarke wasn't very successful, was it?" Myra said when she looked at Costa's record.

"I know. But that's what happens when you're young and you're busy having a good time. School was not a priority for me at all then. It is now."

"That's nice to hear."

"Do you think I'll ever get into university with a record like that?"

"With a record like that, no. Although you probably could get in as a 'mature student', you're old enough and you've been out of school for a few years."

"I know that. But I want to clean up my record, and I want to finish what I once started."

"Okay. But I can tell you that anyone with a little experience knows how to read a transcript. A transcript tells a story, and your story is that you hardly went to class. Students who legitimately fail get forty-sevens and fifty-fives, they don't get sixes and elevens like you did.

"Let's see what kind of high school student you were," Myra said, and she called up Costa's high school record. "Not fantastic, but better. You didn't fail any courses in high school."

"I went to a private school where they kept a close watch on us. When I came here, the freedom got to me, I guess…But that's why I'm back, to prove to myself that I can do it, that I can do better. I know I can."

"So why now, why not last year or the year before? Let's see, you've been away for three—no, four—years."

"Well, I met this girl, and…"

▶ Pietro

Two weeks later Myra met another young man in his early twenties with a similar bad record. He had performed terribly when he had first attended Clarke and he, too, was determined to clean up his record.

"I know I can do it. It hasn't bothered me until now, but it's bothering me now, big time," Pietro said.

"So why is it bothering you now, 'big time'?" Myra asked.

And out came a response similar to Costa's, except in Pietro's case his girlfriend was finishing her degree in kinesiology and had a job lined up in her field as soon as she graduated…

"So if you had to do it all over again, would you do it differently?" Myra asked Pietro.

"Are you kidding me? I would take school much more seriously, I wouldn't waste my time. I know I'll be going to school with students much younger than me, I would like to tell them not to make the same mistake I made."

"I wish you could, too. We try to tell them, but the message goes in one ear and out the other," Myra said. "I met a young man a few weeks ago who is in a situation similar to yours. I wish I could get you both on record and get your message out to all our students."

"I know, I was told to shape up the first time I was here but I ignored the advice. After all, I was eighteen and I thought I knew what I was doing. Oh, well." Pietro shrugged.

When the semester came to an end, Myra checked the records of both young men. They had each gotten in the high eighties or low nineties in all of their courses.

KUDOS

~~~~~

▶ 180-degree Turn

A girlfriend did not set Darren on the right path, he did it all by himself. He, too, had started at Clarke and failed all his courses two semesters in a row. "I was having major issues with my father, I was doing drugs, I was not in the least bit interested in school. I left Montreal after I was kicked out of Clarke. I travelled in Europe, did odd jobs here and there. I was there for about three years.

"After I came back I bounced around some more, but last year I decided to come back to school to pick up where I left off and to do it differently."

"I'll say," Myra said. "Your recent record is impeccable."

"But is it good enough to get into Social Work at McGill?"
~~~~~

"Yes, but you have to call McGill's attention to the difference between before and after. There's a field on the application form for this. We will also recalculate your average without all those early failures. They won't do that, you have to do that for them.

"There is another thing," Myra continued. "Social Work does not admit just according to grades. You need to have some volunteer experience, some community involvement."

"Oh, I have that. I founded a fathers and sons basketball club in the West Island. We rent the gym at a nearby high school and meet every Friday evening. It's a great program. After I came back I reconciled with my father and we came up with an idea together."

"Gosh, Darren. That sounds stupendous. McGill is going to love you."

"You think?"

"I don't think, I know."

"One last question. When's the deadline to apply?"

▶ Plan B

Peter was a student in Clarke's Animal Health program, the program that trains veterinarian assistants. He was doing reasonably well in his program but his ambition was to become a veterinarian.

Peter's science background was not strong, however, and he was missing some high school pre-requisites for the college-level science courses he needed to take to qualify for vet school.

"I love the field," Peter said. "And I also have lots of contacts in the field. But one of the vets I know, although he's encouraging me, told me that he couldn't help me get into vet school, that you either had the grades to get in or you didn't. So that's why I'm here, where do I start?"

"Let's see," Myra said. "You have high school chemistry and some math, but you're missing high school physics and a second math course before you can take the college-level courses you need to get into vet school.

"And, Peter, I have to be frank with you—your high school grades and college grades are not that strong. They're okay, but to get into vet school they have to be more than strong, they have to be super strong. So do you think you can do better, do you think you could get grades in the high eighties, ideally   in the nineties, if you put your mind to it?"

"I think so, except I'm pretty busy these days. I've started a volunteer service for people with mental illness. I read about this and thought that we needed this service in Montreal. It's like the idea of seeing-eye dogs, except in this case you team up specially trained dogs with children who are autistic or people who are suffering from Post-Traumatic Stress Disorder and it seems to help them."

Myra sat back in her chair. "I'm blown away, Peter. That's fantastic, fantastic."

"Well, it had to be done, and I'm good with people and with dogs, so I decided to do it. It's keeping me very, very busy."

"So how will you find the time to do your program, which is demanding in itself, and take your science prerequisites and give them the time they need for you to do well?"

"Well, I want to try. I've always wanted to be a vet and I want to give it a shot."

"Okay. So next semester, I'll register you in a physics course, and we'll take this one step at a time."

Peter came back to see Myra the following semester, a few weeks after classes started. "I'm here to withdraw from my program."

"Oh, no, Peter, what happened? I hope you're all right."

Peter was a very amiable fellow, but this time his smile suffused his whole face. "I got a grant from the government to develop the program I told you about, and I just couldn't turn it down. The service is taking off, we're helping people, I have ideas about how to develop the service further, and for now, that's what I want to do. I just can't keep up with my studies, and to be honest, I don't think, even if I devoted myself fully to them, that I could get the kinds of grades you said I needed. Take a look at this," Peter said, and he handed Myra his business card.

Myra looked at the card then looked back at Peter. "Oh, Peter. I'm so happy for you. You know, I thought about you after our first encounter, about how special your idea was. And you made it happen, you went and made it happen. I feel privileged to know you. My heartiest congratulations. Wow, that's all I can say, wow!"

"Thanks, Miss, thank you." Peter's beam lit up the room.

EPILOGUE

<div style="text-align: center;">~~~</div>

Why I Don't Retire is the I first title I considered when I began compiling the preceding collection of exchanges I had with CEGEP students. If I stayed on in my position as advisor well beyond my retirement years, it was as I said more than once to my partner, my children and my friends, the job was a perfect match for me. I loved explaining things, I loved dealing with young adults, there was hardly any pressure. I did what I had to do within the workday and went home. Unlike teaching high school, my first job after university, when there were always preparations and corrections to do, and unlike admissions, the job I found at Clarke after I left teaching, when I woke up every working day in March, April and May at five o'clock in the morning because there was so much work to do, I would never finish I feared. I always finished but when you are OCD…

I never stopped thanking the goddess for having been good to me, for having led me to this perfect job in a great school, with wonderful colleagues. I can go on and on....

135